MEG'S CHRISTMAS

MW00564809

for Jacquetta

MEG'S CHRISTMAS

Jan Pieńkowski & David Walser

PUFFIN BOOKS

Meg made a spell

The spell took them to a castle

Dinner was served

in the Great Hall

That night nobody slept

Meg, Mog and Owl

They decorated the tree

Goodbye! Happy New Year!